A Note to Parents and Caregivers:

Read-it! Readers are for children who are just starting on the amazing road to reading. These beautiful books support both the acquisition of reading skills and the love of books.

 The PURPLE LEVEL presents basic topics and objects using high frequency words and simple language patterns.

 The RED LEVEL presents familiar topics using common words and repeating sentence patterns.

 The BLUE LEVEL presents new ideas using a larger vocabulary and varied sentence structure.

 The YELLOW LEVEL presents more challenging ideas, a broad vocabulary, and wide variety in sentence structure.

 The GREEN LEVEL presents more complex ideas, an extended vocabulary range, and expanded language structures.

 The ORANGE LEVEL presents a wide range of ideas and concepts using challenging vocabulary and complex language structures.

When sharing a book with your child, read in short stretches, pausing often to talk about the pictures. Have your child turn the pages and point to the pictures and familiar words. And be sure to reread favorite stories or parts of stories.

There is no right or wrong way to share books with children. Find time to read with your child, and pass on the legacy of literacy.

Adria F. Klein, Ph.D.
Professor Emeritus
California State University
San Bernardino, California

For little Adrienne Murphy and both her dads ...

Editor: Christianne Jones
Page Production: Tracy Davies
Creative Director: Keith Griffin
Editorial Director: Carol Jones
Managing Editor: Catherine Neitge

First American edition published in 2006 by
Picture Window Books
5115 Excelsior Boulevard
Suite 232
Minneapolis, MN 55416
877-845-8392
www.picturewindowbooks.com

First published in Canada in 2001 by
Les éditions Héritage inc.
300 Arran Street, Saint Lambert
Quebec, Canada J4R 1K5

Printed in the United States of America.

Library of Congress Cataloging-in-Publication Data
Tibo, Gilles.
Alex and Sarah / by Gilles Tibo ; illustrated by Philippe Germain.
p. cm. — (Read-it! readers)
Summary: When Sarah loses the hockey ball in a scary dog's backyard, Alex figures
out a clever way to get it back so that the game can continue.
ISBN 1-4048-1352-7 (hard cover)
[1. Hockey—Fiction. 2. Dogs—Fiction.] I. Germain, Philippe, 1963- ill. II. Title.
III. Series.

PZ7.T433Ag 2005
[E]—dc22
                                                    2005003737

Alex
and Sarah

by Gilles Tibo
illustrated by Philippe Germain

Special thanks to our advisers for their expertise:

Adria F. Klein, Ph.D.
Professor Emeritus, California State University
San Bernardino, California

Susan Kesselring, M.A.
Literacy Educator
Rosemount–Apple Valley–Eagan (Minnesota) School District

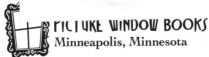

PICTURE WINDOW BOOKS
Minneapolis, Minnesota

Hi!

I play hockey like my friend Alex. I'm a goalie. I trap pucks with a big catching glove. Yesterday, I made an incredible save with my glove! At the end of the first period, my friend Brian scored the first goal.

When the second period started, the other team shot the puck high into the corner of the net. I made another incredible save!

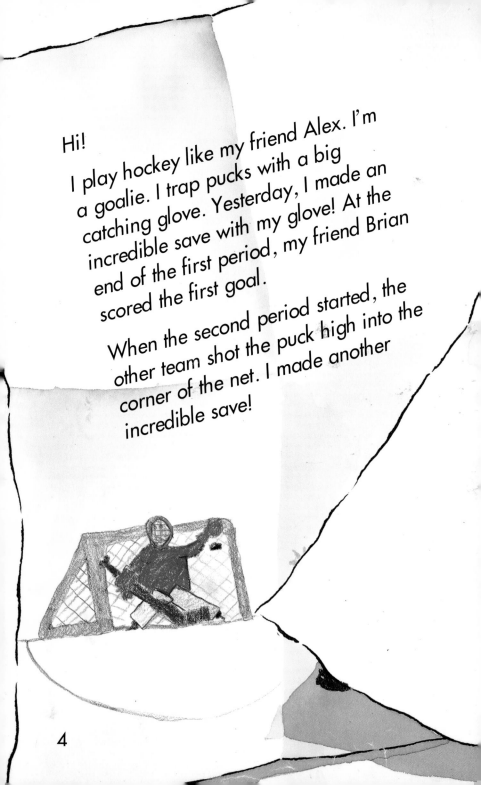

The game went on ... and on. Both goalies stopped all the pucks hit at them.

In the third period, both teams each scored a goal. The blast of the horn finally ended the game. We won 2-1. Everybody was so proud of me! Being a good goalie is really important. You have to watch carefully and concentrate hard.

Tony Houle
age 8

My name is Alex. This is my
new hockey jersey. See, I'm
number 4.

I put on my cool jersey, and
I practice my shots in the alley.
My dog Toolie and I are getting
ready for the game on Saturday.
I plan to score 100 goals in the
first period, 200 goals in the
second period, and 300 goals
in the third period!

On Saturday morning, I count the players on my team. One of them is missing. Matthew, the left winger, is sick and can't play. Now what are we going to do?

I see Sarah riding by on her bike. Sarah is really cool. I ask her to join my team. I lend her a stick. Before the game starts, I show her a few of my secret hockey moves.

The game starts. Since we're playing outside, we use a ball instead of a puck. I pass the ball to Joel, and he passes it to Sarah. Sarah's all alone, right in front of the other team's goalie!

She shoots ... and ... doesn't score! The ball bounces off the net and lands on the other side of the neighbor's fence.

We take a look through the boards of the fence. Oh no! We see the neighbor's mean dog, Mack. He has big sharp teeth and a loud bark. There's no way we can get the ball back!

Discouraged, we try to play with an old balloon. One minute into the game, the balloon bursts.

We try to play with an old tin can. Two minutes later, big Simon crushes it under his foot.

We try to play with an old pot. Toolie gets his paw stuck in it.

We try to play with a big pebble, but it hurts too bad. There's no way we can go on like this.

We have tried everything.

Sarah says, "I've got an idea. Let's go ask Mack's owner. He'll give us back the ball!"

We walk around the block and ring the doorbell at the front door. No one answers. We ring again. The owner isn't home. Mack is alone in the backyard.

We go back to the alley. I really, really,
really want to play. I want to score 100
goals, 200 goals, and 300 goals! I have
to figure out a plan.

I have an idea. I tie three hockey sticks together, end-to-end. Then I slip the sticks between the boards of the fence. The big dog growls. He gnaws at the sticks. He chews them into 100, 200, 300 pieces!

Sarah dashes home and comes back
with a long metal pipe. She slips the
pipe between the boards of the fence.
The big dog barks. When he tries to bite
the pipe, he kicks the ball away with his
paw. It rolls even further out of reach.
There's no way to get it back now.

Then, I get a brilliant idea.

"Sarah, come with me.
Everyone else wait here!"
I tell my friends.

Sarah and I run home. I rummage through the fridge for a sausage. Sarah rummages through the closet for some rope.

Smiling, I say, "Just wait until you see this!"

Sarah and I run back to our friends. They stare at me in amazement.

"What are you going to do?" they ask.

"You'll see," I say with a smile.

I tie the rope to the end of the pipe. I tie the sausage to the end of the rope. Then, I climb up on the fence. I slowly move the sausage over the fence.

Mack sees the sausage and follows it across the yard. Quickly, Toolie runs through a small hole in the fence.

"Hurry up, Toolie! Get the ball!" I yell.

While Mack is finishing off the sausage at the other end of the yard, Toolie latches onto the ball. Quickly, he runs back.

"Great idea," Sarah says. "Alex,
you are so cool!"

27

We start the game again, but I sit down on the bench. Sarah gives me a big smile. She's ready to play.

Our team loses the game 6-0. Sarah says,
"I don't care if we lose. I play for fun.
How about you, Alex?"

"Uhh … me, too … I just play for fun, too …"
I say with a smile.

31

More *Read-it!* Readers

Bright pictures and fun stories help you practice your reading skills. Look for more books at your level.

Alex and Sarah by Gilles Tibo
Alex and the Team Jersey by Gilles Tibo
Alex and Toolie by Gilles Tibo
Clever Cat by Karen Wallace
Felicio's Incredible Invention by Mireille Villeneuve
Flora McQuack by Penny Dolan
Izzie's Idea by Jillian Powell
Mysteries for Felicio by Mireille Villeneuve
Naughty Nancy by Anne Cassidy
Parents Do the Weirdest Things! by Louise Tondreau-Levert
Peppy, Patch, and the Bath by Marisol Sarrazin
Peppy, Patch, and the Postman by Marisol Sarrazin
Peppy, Patch, and the Socks by Marisol Sarrazin
The Princess and the Frog by Margaret Nash
The Roly-Poly Rice Ball by Penny Dolan
Run! by Sue Ferraby
Sausages! by Anne Adeney
Stickers, Shells, and Snow Globes by Dana Meachen Rau
Theodore the Millipede by Carole Tremblay
The Truth About Hansel and Gretel by Karina Law
Willie the Whale by Joy Oades

Looking for a specific title or level? A complete list of *Read-it!* Readers is available on our Web site:
www.picturewindowbooks.com